Lies Over the

Martha Lane

abuddhapress@yahoo.co

ISBN: 9798390396018

Alien Buddha Press 2023

®™©

Martha Lane 2023

The following is a work of fiction. Any similarities to actual people, places, or events, unless deliberately expressed otherwise by the author are purely coincidental.

i.

The waves spat red onto the sand. The surf's bubbles were thick with blood. A soup. No one could see the source. Where it was coming from. How it was still coming. It was impossible to tell. Water and seaweed churned and dispersed the gore until it was no more. In less than a minute the tide devoured the scene. Onlookers gathered in the shallows, checked around their ankles for clues. Desperate not to find anything. Thea watched the crowd as her bare feet slapped against the wet sand. The clump of people stood out on the slowly darkening bay. The beach tried to swallow her every step, dragging at her heels. She choked on the iron-rich mist. The sea was loud. Not crashing, but a constant low roll of thunder. She sped up.

  Maybe it was a bird? A diving bird, crescent moon wings, struck a rock, confused by the children shouting. Perhaps someone had cut themselves on an urchin. The chatter fizzed with ideas to explain what had happened. What had they seen? Nothing much. No one was putting their head under the water though, and no one was willing to talk about the metallic tang in the air. The taste of pennies hanging on the fret.

Thea had no desire to confirm what she already knew. What made the knotted tangle of scars at her elbow tingle and itch. What was going to cause her endless hours of unpaid overtime tomorrow. She started a second lap of the bay with a heavy pant, remembering the cooler October months of her childhood. When running alone would not have staved the chill. A jumper often not enough, she'd have had a thin cagoule on too. Wrestled into the shiny luminescent thing by her parents. She wasn't even sure if you could buy those anymore. Why would you need to?

She headed towards the cluster of bathers about half a mile down the shore. They were oblivious to the commotion near the rockpools, so they still splashed and whooped in the gentle rise and fall of the swell. Thea wondered how long it would take the ripple of stillness to spread over the entire beach. With each attack it got longer. The public were growing immune to them. Like watching war footage on the TV. So certain it couldn't affect them, they grew in confidence every day they didn't become prey. Pretending not to notice that the UK had long overtaken Australia and South Africa, and was advancing, streamlined towards US numbers of fatal attacks was a daily pastime for most. As ingrained as brushing their teeth. Thing is, 1,000 a year from a populace the size of the States could be swept aside as untroubling, 'more risk in your car than in the sea'. That many a year from the UK and it wouldn't be long before everyone knew someone who had been attacked by a shark.

She tried to concentrate on the lecture coming through her headphones and ignore the growl of the sea.

ii.

The clouds rolled in; Thea decided to stop her run short. A new group of beach goers passed by in wetsuits. Actively waiting for the sky to turn purple before they took their dive. Besides avoiding the water, which seemed impossible for some. Those who felt the tide in their veins, who were as part of the sea as the salt. The only way to guarantee a safe passage from the sharks, was to swim during an electrical storm. When the bruised sky fizzed and crackled. When, inland, great forks of lightening hurled themselves at the earth. Fireworks of mud and rock exploding, trees splitting in two; the cracks of the wood sending shudders to the roots. When, at the coast, great sheets of electricity fell from the sky. Forks so close together they were completely indistinguishable from one another. Blinding. They rustled like a lace curtain. Lace weaved to wound. Hillsides of dry heather set ablaze while the sea boiled. When doors had to be bolted against hot high winds and windows were lined with lead sheets. When kestrels circled, unable to settle. When dogs barked at the air that was about to bark back. When the sombre cries of terns fell with a thud against clouds so thick, they sagged.

The animals could sense it in the water, the pressure building, started vacating hours before the sparks rained. Only the jellyfish stayed, unable to swim away. Blooms of soft bodies suspended in the brine, glowing in the light show. Creatures from sharks to guppies fled to calmer coasts, Northern France, the Netherlands. Thea's sea became as deserted as a graveyard. Those caught in rockpools ran the risk of being electrocuted in their homes, as the pools became conductors for currents too unwieldy for the atmosphere.

And still, some people felt safer swimming when the surf lost control and the horizon caught fire.

iii.

Thea fiddled with her earbuds, wanted the radio. Something mindless to accompany her on the walk back. A song she recognised burst through the speakers. She saw her mother dancing in the kitchen. She saw her father stomping home in the rain. She saw the mud slide away, steal half of their house as it went. Felt her knees buckle.

No one mourned the loss. The loss of the ground beneath their feet as the ocean tore away chunks of the land, gnashing with salt spray saliva drooling. No one spoke about losing more animal species than there had been dinosaurs, of the lives they'd lived so freely before, of the countless unnamed people who just weren't there anymore. Displaced and confined to a hidden history for the authorities. No one felt able to use their voice, to complain, instead with each mini disaster it was instilled into them, from TV screens, billboards, radio announcements, that this was the time to simply pull together. Find positivity, move forward. It was only when a select few started to look back that they saw the full scale of the destruction. Wished they'd paid more attention when the daisies bloomed one November. The planet was wounded. Irreparably.

The trees had screamed for it to stop; their blackened leaves dropped, their fruit rotten and sour. The sea changed shape and its flavour. The wind changed direction, blew with a ferocity that was biblical. Time was harder to measure as the seasons blurred. Volcanoes rose, belched the fire in their bellies so it rained. Scorched more than the earth. Icebergs shrank, rivers shrank, lakes disappeared. The droughts came, announced by tornadoes. They ransacked and pillaged. Stole so much.

Nevertheless, humans hoped. Endeavoured. Survived. They had to. It was in their DNA. Survival was key. Without processing their grief, they started to rebuild. Everyone working doggedly, fuelled by the pretence they were perfectly fine.

iv.

At home, Thea tossed her damp running gear next to the laundry basket. Lightening flashed through her window. The glass rattled in response.

'Kids! Why hasn't the washing been done?'

Silence.

She blew a raspberry at no one. Calling them kids was doing them a favour. She could forgive a child for not cleaning up after themselves, as she frequently had done. For years, playing skivvy to their every whim. Somehow, she had found herself with two near-adults in her home, who were unable to manage even the most basic of household functions. She picked up the lycra she'd just peeled from herself and hand washed it in the sink. Squeezing tightly to wring out the water and stench.

She turned up the temperature on the shower, trying to melt the thoughts of the beach from her. She thought of the family, beginning to wonder why their loved one hadn't returned home. Maybe this wasn't the first time they'd felt the rising fear. Felt uncertainty washed away by the brute force of hard terrible facts, like bullets. Puncture wounds left behind by the biting truth.

No one could exactly recall the first time, maybe not even the first ten or twenty. But at some point, everybody agreed that it was something to be concerned about. Warnings of warming water were ignored for so long by the time people had caught up, they weren't warnings anymore. One tone of voice workshop and the messages became marketing. The North Sea was branded a new haven for spa lovers and sun worshippers.

The warm water brought money before it brought sharks.

The first attacks were provoked. Men mainly, who wanted to regale others with the time they'd punched a maneater in the face. Square in the jaw. Teeth couldn't stop them. A smarter man might have done his research, learnt the length of a pup. Learnt that even if provoked a Hammerhead does little damage. Those more in need of props for their masculinity, went in with kitchen blades and aimed for the eyes. The sharks, vexed by the attacks, fast learnt that they were bigger, stronger, swifter, and they outnumbered the bathers. The sharks learnt to bite before bitten. They were indiscriminate. Unfortunately, humans did not, could not, or refused to, learn anything.

Maimed bodies became the norm.

V.

Those who governed waited for one too many attacks. A grandmother protecting her grandson, neither survived. Nor did the lifeguard who leapt onto his jet-ski, racing straight into the gaping jaws of danger. It was a story the media ran with for months. It instilled a fear not held towards the ocean since the 1970s, before even Thea's Grandparents' childhoods. Nobody was going beyond ankle deep into the water.

Thea had been a child that summer, spent her time paddling, watching for fins in the distance, wondering why that wasn't enough for people. Why did they need to go deeper? She watched from the beach, sand scorching her toes, as the huge complex appeared, what seemed to her, overnight. The white panels floated in the sky, suspended by cranes that dwarfed the wind turbines, and were slotted into place. The roof looked like a ballet dancer's tutu, or the ruffled wing of a dove.

The Oceanic Research Centre of Accord was built.

The institute was designed to make the water safe again, to find a way in which sharks and people could live harmoniously (in a way people could continue to live their lives without changing a single thing). To begin with they gave daily briefings, wanted the public to know all the hard work they were putting in to finding a cure. A cure for sharks. The oldest living creature on the planet.

This worked until leaked footage of the test sharks flooded the press, with their half-peeled skin and their white cloudy eyes. The pups born with six fins, bent fins, no fins. It worked better for everyone if the public remained ignorant. Breakthroughs were reported and day-to-day progress was left to the imagination.

It took them years to realise that while the public relied on science, they did not believe a word the scientists said. What people seemed to crave was a well-presented speaker, someone smart but not alienating, who made them feel at ease. A young woman who looked healthy, like she ran laps on the beach, and who spoke the same language as them. Lab coats reminded them too much of the sharks they wanted very much to avoid

vi.

Thea stifled a yawn, behind the back of her hand. The scent of lemons wafted in through an open window. It was a scent as synonymous with the North now as it had been with the islands of Sicily in her mother's childhood. There was a polaroid of her Mam as a girl, clutching large sunshine-coloured fruits in pudgy hands. It used to hang at an angle, on the front of the fridge. Fading in the sunlight that had steadily grown stronger through their kitchen. As the ground in Palermo charred and the plants withered, England had become the place to visit if you wanted to smell citrus on the breeze. A scent now as expensive as gold.

    The trees were safe in the complex, lining the buildings. The grounds had security guards, and high-wired fences, barbed and electrified. The lawns were small but always immaculate. And behind the buildings, the river. Flowing where institute machinery told it to. They were close enough to the ocean that the water was still salty. A seal or otter could sometimes be spotted scurrying away from huge ferries blaring their way out to sea. The port was once used for fishing and ship building. Thea's generation grew up listening to the stories of their grandparents who were really relaying their own grandparents' stories. A time of hard graft, oil and sweat. A time of few resources, yet spirit in abundance. Apparently. Sounded exhausting.

The outside of the building was lined with sepia photos, enlarged and printed on hoardings, of this bygone era. The landscape unrecognisable from the one locals trod today. The beach of Thea's childhood didn't exist anymore, metallic beasts had pulled down the dunes, flattened them once the rising tide had taken too much of the holiday makers' favoured spots. Instead of gentle slopes to the sand which Thea had once toddled slowly down, reaching for an adult's hand on the worn-out concrete steps, and where loose sand threatened to slip under foot, a stark cliff face. Smooth like a dam. That was now the abrupt end to your day at the beach.

She snapped back to the bright white room, to the table of expectant faces. They'd asked something, needed an answer. She hated these meetings. The scientists in their crisp doctor's coats, knew she didn't have the medical expertise to follow every part of the conversations. Knew she was there through sheer luck, not quite nepotism. Knew she had as many skills they didn't possess, as they did that were alien to her. They never fully gave in to their distaste though. Aware she was the face of their business. Wary of a woman who had lost so much. Wary of a woman who chose not to rebuild missing limbs. Wary of a woman who it was said, let her own children be used in the name of science.

    She smiled sweetly and asked for them to repeat the question. Not one rolled their eyes at the marketer who somehow owned them all.

vii.

Leaving school was all Thea had ever wanted to do. She hadn't ever thought much beyond stepping out of the doors. Spilling out into the streets she'd grown up on, the streets lined with Georgian houses and pubs named after sea shanties no one knew the words to anymore. But as an adult. Someone to direct rather than be directed. She was smart, did as she was told, a model student. But she'd felt trapped. Wanted desperately to leave.

She'd found an office job, as if there was any other type of job. Admin suited her, keeping things in order. But it was never good enough to be excellent at administration. No one was ever allowed to flourish in admin without being syphoned off by another department. And communications found Thea. She had a knack for knowing what an audience wanted to hear, and what they needed to hear, and how to marry the two when they weren't necessarily the same thing.

She'd applied for the job at O.R.C.A. on a whim. Was drawn to the infamy, drawn to the prospect of travel, wondered how involved she would be with the creatures themselves. She'd always walked the long way home, along the seafront, eyes glued to the vast featureless blue, in the hope she'd spot something lurking in the deep. A fin, a splash, a shadow passing through a wave. Or a hunt, where a slick of bodies would curl around each other like tadpoles. She wasn't exactly an animal lover, but she was drawn to these creatures who'd survived this long on an unforgiving planet steered by billions of unforgiving captains.

Her first day she'd been led past the tanks, watched the sharks mill aimlessly in the water. Their senses dulled, their heads occasionally shaking, trying to awaken whatever was lost inside them. What had been taken from them. She was outnumbered by those who wore lab coats, unable to do her job without their brains, their incredible way of seeing the world, she was at their mercy. But it was she who was invited into the CEO's office. Who instantly moved through the building, apex in ambition. It did not take long before she ran the marketing department, absorbed communications and advertising. Internal and external. Thea became O.R.C.A.'s voice and her word was final.

viii.

'I know you don't want me conducting press conferences anymore,' Thea didn't see the point in sugar-coating or metaphors. The thing she'd been best at, she'd destroyed. She had become the living embodiment of what people feared. How could the public trust the company if they couldn't even keep their own safe.

'Unless you're willing to lie about how it happened?' A Board member wafted his hand in the direction of her arm.

'I am a marketer,' she smiled.

A ripple of polite laughter made its way across the table.

'A big jacket, no one would even notice.'

She could not agree.

'This is my community, James, people know me. They already know what happened. They also know why.' Her heart pounded, clattered against her ribs. She breathed in through her nose. 'We've always been honest here. Now isn't the time to change that.'

Uncomfortable shuffles erupted.

'Saying that, we don't have to give out every minute detail. Me and the team will post a statement. People will be invited to donate in,' she swallowed hot bile, 'in Hector's name.'

A few nods.

'Are you happy to just leave this to me?'

Stronger nods. Of course they were.

ix.

Staring at her dirty feet, Thea lamented the thick-skinned heels. Her whole life she'd promoted the exfoliating nature of sand. She couldn't remember the last time she hadn't spent part of her day on the beach, but it didn't seem to be working. Maybe she should start wearing shoes round the house, buy some of those little cotton socks to wear with shea butter in bed. Even the thought bored her.

'Does that sound plausible?'

Thea looked up. Dr Reinau's pencil hovered over his notebook, waiting to analyse. To delve into her unconscious being. She opened her mouth, ready to blag some lie, but that was a risky strategy in this office. She uncrossed her legs and slipped her feet back inside her sandals. Backless, two straps across the top, with large buckles. The kind Mam would have worn, confined to the summer months. When there were still four seasons.

'I wasn't listening.'

'That's very honest of you.'

'Surely you could tell?'

'Naturally. But others might have said "could you repeat the question?" or "sorry, I didn't quite catch that" for fear of reproach.'

'You can't tell me off, I'm not a child.' Thea fought the urge to throw her arm across her chest.

The pencil started scribbling.

'You don't think as a doctor I have the right to scold you, if it's for your own good? Would a cardiologist not reprimand a man who continued to eat red meat after a bypass?'

'Scold away. But if all that man needed was a chiding to stop him, I suspect the operation would definitely be enough to dissuade him from having a burger.'

Dr Reinau stopped writing and took his glasses off. He looked at her with sympathetic eyes. Eyes the colour of rain clouds.

'Did you argue?'

Thea's mouth turned to dust, she scratched her head and exhaled, 'if you think this is arguing.'

Undeterred, 'did you spar?'

'I don't see how this is about my arm.'

'It's about loss.'

'Trying to be a cardiologist and fix my broken heart?' Her voice cracked eggshell.

X.

Hunched over the desk, Hector was writing his letter. Thea watched from the doorway, savouring the cool tiles under her toes. Mila was struggling with the water filter in the kitchen, cropped hair tucked behind her ears. A pixie cut for their pixie. A girl born to be the big fish, Thea worried constantly about her not pushing, not challenging herself, not attempting to swim in bigger ponds where she might not be the star attraction.

She didn't look up as she shouted through to her father, 'it's so morbid you know?'

Hector folded the letter and posted it into his top drawer.

'Al contrario,' he called back.

'Sí lo es.'

Mila's Spanish had always made Thea smile, fluent and round and drenched in sunshine, leap frogging over her Geordie lilt.

Hector stood and stretched. His shirt untucking itself and revealing a soft downy stomach. He neatened everything on his desk then turned to face his fire-fuelled daughter.

'I just rest easier knowing that if anything *were* to happen to me then your mama would know where everything was. Passwords, bank accounts, bodies.' He smiled at Thea and placed a hand on her hip, leaned in for a kiss which she playfully ducked away from.

'Why don't you know that already?' Mila turned to her mother with a finger pointing, loaded with accusation.

'Hey. This has nothing to do with feminism. I know all that stuff for O.R.C.A., I think it's just fine your dad does it for us.'

'Plus, I enjoy ripping it up every time I do return in one piece.' Hector winked and picked up his bag.

'It's tuna steaks for tea.'

'There's my reason for coming home then.'

xi.

Thea tutted as she saw Hector's blue shirt, the print of tiny fingernail-sized sharks that he thought was hilarious to wear to conferences and talks. She couldn't remember the last time she'd seen him in it. Meant it had been there for weeks, 'drying'. She picked it up and went to hang it in the wardrobe. There was a knock at the door. Unannounced visitors weren't really a staple of the house. The kids always arranged meetings with their friends with a tirade of messages first. She padded down the stairs, still clutching the coat hanger, half draped in cotton.

It was one of the biologists from the complex. His name escaped her, but she recognised him. He was wearing a branded hoodie, the type the divers took out with them to stay warm on the boat. He looked flushed. His hair was wet. Understanding dawned on Thea like waves knocking against a hull.

Hector.

Accident.

Dead.

The man said that he was sorry. Explained that it was a faulty tube. There may have been a puncture.

'Shark bite?'

He shifted uncomfortably. She didn't care what the answer was anyway. Whatever had caused the tear, whether it was a mako or a splintered cleat. What did it matter? The end result was the same. Hector had drowned. Drowned a metre below the boat in position to keep him safe.

She pushed past the man, whose own eyes swam with tears, leaving her door open, and still holding on to Hector's shirt.

She ran to the sand. To the sea. To the last place he had smiled and laughed and thought and breathed. She ran into the water, slowly and clumsily as she smashed into the waves with her body. The shirt got away, wrenched from her hand by the chomping white surf. She screamed then. A noise so loud and sharp it clawed at her throat. A noise that ripped open the orange sky and shook the seabed. Then she started to swim. She thrashed her way towards the sunset. Towards where the boat had spent the day. She didn't pause even when her breathe became ragged.

The tip of a tail cut the surface and flicked from side to side. She stopped to tread water and screamed again. Her rage seemed to feed the soft swell, made the waves mountains. She slapped her arms against the surface of the water.

'You bastard.'

'Come.'

'Come on.'

The dorsal fin changed direction. Attracted to the splashes, to the noise. The tell-tale signs of a creature in distress whipped up all a shark's prehistoric urges. Its streamlined body fuelled purely by instinct as it ducked under the water. The rage bled from her, fast like an artery had been severed.

She had to get out. Her world started to spin. A merry-go-round she hadn't meant to get on.

As slowly and gently as she could, she pulled herself through the water, gliding. She glanced back to the shore. It seemed further away. She tried to concentrate on making herself streamlined. Not on how stupid she felt. Not on how her rising fear was making the water around her pulse.

The fin, so much bigger now, appeared at her side. Sliced the surface. Moses parting the not-yet-red sea. The triangle disappeared as it sunk under the waves. Underneath her.

xii.

Pulled to the left.

    Bashed from the right.

    She was dragged down.

    Pushed up with a fierce speed.

    Rocket fast.

    Inhaling water like it was air.

    Inhaling air like it was lemon zest.

    Thrown aside.

    Devoured.

    Pain like no other.

    Pain like all others.

    Pain easily pinpointed.

    Pain hard to describe.

    She fought.

    Tugged herself free.

    In pieces.

    She was lost.

    Driftwood.

xiii.

Thea was tossed onto the beach. She gasped and coughed. The water around her was crimson and clotted. The salted foam tinged with her.

'Help,' she whispered.

'Help.'

Sand grated against her cheeks and tongue. Wet sticky seaweed clung to her stomach and thighs. She was too tired to move them. Too lacking even for that. She closed her eyes. She didn't have time to consider her terrible mistake before her nose and mouth were covered by the next rush of the hungry tide.

xiv.

The boat barely moved, just a gentle roll. Thea moved her feet slightly to steady herself. No one around her was holding on, they looked as comfortable as they would on tarmac. They chatted relaxed, completely ignored her. Couldn't figure out why someone from corporate needed to be in their domain. She didn't mention that Hector had asked her to come. Didn't mention that she'd jumped at the chance.

'It's a millpond,' Hector winked, happy to be sharing a private joke with her. He had pulled himself into his wetsuit. She concentrated on maintaining eye contact. Hoped the rose blossoming on her cheeks wasn't too noticeable. Since the night at the pub, they hadn't spent time together outside of work. She had been losing hope, starting to think she'd misread something, when he asked her to join him on today's trip. The team needed to tag pups to help them determine the rate of population growth. The boats were setting sail daily.

Fins scythed the water, chopping the rolls where waves might be. Someone was scattering chum. She was desperate to disguise the wretch that was climbing up her gullet. Coughed, hummed, anything. The pups threw themselves against one another, fighting for the easy food. To her left, Hector slid into the water. Barely caused a ripple. An expert, he swept them up by their tails, rolled them onto their backs. They became docile immediately, clay at the touch of his fingertips.

Only when he pulled himself back onto the deck did Thea realise, she'd been holding her breath. He removed his goggles, the lines in the corners of his eyes creased as he looked up at her.

'Glad to have you back on board.'

He held out his cold wet hand, she pulled him up. She fell hard in that instant when their eyes became level. She forgot to let go.

XV.

In a hospital bed, Thea threw her clammy head across the pillow. Hector, just out of reach was trying to talk but wouldn't. Couldn't. Afraid of what she might see, Thea tried to run but she kept twisting, changing direction. There was no path, just shifting sand. Dune mountains sprouted and fell. The rumble of diggers and the screech of saws battled for space in her head. She thought she could smell burning but then she was underwater. She was swimming against the tide, dorsal fins everywhere. Hector was still just out in front. Walking. She tried to walk but there was no ground.

Hector.

She called again.

You're not listening to me.

At that, Hector finally stopped. He turned and embraced her. Squeezed her. Loved her. Before she could say no, he spun her round, arm arched for her to drift under. He kept spinning her while his soundless mouth continued to talk. Dizzy, Thea felt vomit threatening.

Stop.

I can't hear you.

Hector kept her twirling until it was just her.

He was gone.

xvi.

Mila was leaning back in the hospital chair, cross-legged, foot twitching. She wouldn't sit still. She wouldn't look away from the window. Hadn't given her mother one glance since she'd arrived. Thea understood. When she'd woken, even before her eyes were fully open, she knew that the children had been told about their father. The air was spiced with grief. Tasted like liquorice. Pressed heavy on her eyelids. For a fraction of a second, she'd contemplated pretending to sleep for a few moments longer. But the conversation wouldn't be any easier in half an hour. She owed her kids more than a feigned snore and a flicker of her eyelashes.

    Xavier was by her bedside, conjured a worried smile. His hand was on her sheets, as close to her skin as physically possible without touching it. Looked like his dad. Thea scrunched her eyes back together. Couldn't face him.

    'What were you thinking?' Mila whispered.

    'I'm sorry.' A whisper made of gravel.

    'You went looking for the sharks, didn't you?' Xavier this time.

Thea nodded. Unable to say how ridiculous she felt. How guilt ripped at her like barbed wire.

'You were going to leave us alone.'

That wasn't a question.

xvii.

'You up to this?' Thea asked both of her children as she adjusted her sling, too bright against the granite-grey woollen dress she wore. That's what they looked like today, children. Too young for this.

Me neither.

She'd heard them bickering about who had to sit next to her in the car, who'd have to hold her hand if she cried. That's what Dad's job should have been.

They wore black, had polished their shoes, brushed their hair back. Everything their father would've hated.

'Just stay as long as you can manage.'

Xavier left the room.

He didn't come back.

xviii.

Close up in the mirror, Thea was preoccupied by the cloud of silver hairs that was appearing round her temples. One step back and the greys became far from the most noticeable thing about her. They'd built her a new arm. The doctors and robotics professors. Prosthetics now far surpassed any science fiction she'd read as a child. The brain and the arm spoke to each other somehow. The 'skin' was practically the perfect shade, almost identical to any other part of her. The range of movement greater than her real working hand. Double jointed and strong.

This amazing feat of engineering – and the most expensive thing Thea had ever owned – spent its days leaning against the corner of her bedroom. She didn't use it and never had. Weeks of rehab wasted.

Dr Reinau liked to grill her about it. He suspected she was punishing herself. It was her own fault that she had lost her arm. Why should she make it easier for herself now it was gone? She looked at her whole self in the mirror. She wore a stiff skirt made from wax fabric, down to the knee. Its orange and blue pattern brash against a man's white short sleeved shirt.

A man.

Her stump protruded. It would never matter how brightly coloured her clothes. That would always be the first thing anyone noticed.

'You could wear long sleeves and tuck it in?' As though he could read her mind, Xav appeared behind her. She could see him looking at her arm, not hiding his stares. Not repulsed but not pleased. While Mila still held her entirely accountable for her actions that day, Xavier held her in nothing but grim admiration. Glad that he was not the topic of conversation anymore. A quiet boy with no interest in social rules or expectations he was often misdiagnosed by people who hadn't been asked, as neurodivergent. Perhaps a touch of autism, they would say with a tilted head and a sad little look in their eyes. Thea grew weary of explaining that it was just his way and he didn't need a label. She never suspected he was autistic, just content in his dislike of social settings, and unflinching in his ability to not care what others thought or expected.

In their refusal to seek a diagnosis people saw defiance. Or conspiracy. It had been Thea's strategy to create a good relationship with the community from the pulpit of the giant facility that looked like it had been lifted straight out of a J.J. Abrams film. Placed exactly where the town's aquarium had once been. Where their cranes had built new riverbanks. People shared rumours that Xavier was so docile, so ill-equipped to speak to them because she, the mother who had raised him and loved him since he was a twisted bean right at the core of her, had allowed him to be given the drugs his father was making for the sharks. Wouldn't you want docile well-behaved children if you were a busy working woman? The same could be said for a busy scientific genius father, but when they walked down the street, it wasn't Hector who was met with cold eyes and side steps.

It had been Xav himself who suggested they didn't stop the rumour mill. It might not be a bad thing for competitors and employees to think she was cold enough to inject her own son with a drug so potent it was designed to rewire brains forged long before the dinosaurs, in a darkness so absolute it roared and a depth so overwhelming it bit.

xix.

Grapes had to be cut into eight. Not quartered and quartered again; but sliced. Thinly, fanned around the edge of the plate. Xavier sat on the booster cushion that let him join the family dinner table. He screamed that he was hungry for grapes the whole time he threw them against their dining room wall. Fed up with picking up discarded fruit pulp from the floor, Thea had lost her cool and slammed a bowl in front of her young son.

'You cut them then.'

With a blunt plastic knife, he'd started to cut his food, awkwardly with juice running down his forearms and dripping onto his shorts. He ate so many grapes that day.

Hector watched like he watched his animals. Intensely, intently, silent and thoughtful.

'Clever boy.' Hector's voice was low, calm. Warm. He stroked his son's hair.

Thea slumped on the chair, wiped Mila's face of the tomato stain that was taking over. Stuck her tongue out and waggled her fingers. Mila copied.

'Treat?' Her inflection so high there would definitely be a joke about dolphins brewing in Hector's mind.

Thea stood to retrieve a biscuit, there were only three left. She crammed two into her mouth before anyone could see. She handed Mila the remaining one. Before she'd taken a bite, she had melted chocolate over her hands, face and clothes.

Thea was mid-sigh when Hector squeezed her elbow, kissed her forehead, inhaled.

'Did you save me one?'

'I'll buy more tomorrow.'

'I'll go now if you like? Save you a job?'

His dark brown eyes smiled, he genuinely thought he was being helpful. Her own eyes filled with salt. Begging him not to make her say the words.

Don't leave me alone with them.

'I'll stay. We don't need biscuits right now.'

'Biscuit?' Xav swallowed his last grape slice and held out an expectant hand.

XX.

'People are such a cliché.'

Mila's voice came out of the freezer, she was holding up a container of something slurry-like, caught in the no man's land between red and brown. Their home still brimmed with the food parcels brought by the neighbours in those first few weeks. Their portions of lasagne and broths seasoned with unspoken words. If they'd been lucky Thea had answered the door, hair uncombed, body unwashed, wrapped tightly in Hector's dressing gown. Plenty got Mila or Xavier, who didn't hide the fact they saw the stream of visitors as an unwelcome interruption to their day of avoiding housework, bickering, and using their father's death as an excuse. It probably was, of course Thea knew that, but she didn't want to hear it.

'People were trying to be kind.' Thea was sitting at the table sipping peppermint tea. It was too hot to drink really but the thought of not being preoccupied with something for even a second haunted her. So, she poured scalding water down her throat, would pick at the scabs on her lips for days after.

'Couldn't they be kind with alcohol?' Mila eyed the sludge as if it were roadkill. She lifted the lid, tried to sniff past the whiff of ice. The freezer light burst into rays around her, casting her shadow across the room, long enough that it reached Thea's feet. She reached out, stroked the shadow's head with her slipper.

'Shut the door, sweet. It's Baltic in here.'

'Shame Dad didn't own any thicker night clothes.' Her daughter said, not too unkindly, and squeezed Thea's shoulder as she left the room. Leaving her to look down at Hector's tartan pyjamas, thin cotton kissing her ankles.

xxi.

They blinked and it was winter. Thea hadn't been counting the days but there were five red letters demanding payment on Hector's desk. Every time one had landed on their sand-crusted door mat she'd picked it up without opening and dropped it gently on the desk, dispersing that month's new layer of dust. Today, she sat with the letter as it dropped. Ran her hands over the leather wrapped chair arms and wished they were still warm. The room, unused and unheated, was bitter. Her breath flowered in front of her. She fiddled with the heater, but nothing. Just the click click click of the switch. No whir of a generator or flick of a flame. They'd been cut off. About time. She had been draining the last of their reserves, saved from their solar panel roof. Hoping they'd last longer if she simply closed the doors on the rooms she'd no need for, stop them sucking the heat. But they were vampire rooms, always hungry. With heavy fingers she opened the top drawer where she knew Hector's letter was. Still untouched by anyone other than him.

  Carefully she opened the thing. Paper doesn't retain smell, she checked. The letter was brief. A simple list of numbers to call, passwords to accounts that were linked to his fingerprints, and companies that would hound her for money. That were already hounding. That didn't care that her world had been bulldozed. It didn't matter that the letter was devoid of romance. The fact he wrote it was affection enough. One last act of caregiving in his tall, slanted writing. The last words he wrote. His beautiful name at the bottom of the page with one perfectly symmetrical kiss. She dropped the envelope as she hugged the letter to her chest. She didn't care she was a cliché. She would be a widow by formula if she wanted. The envelope dropped fast and landed with a thunk. There was something else in there.

    She tipped it out into the palm of her hand. It was an old-style key, with teeth and a thumb-sized bulb at the end. She turned over the letter and saw in Spanish, scrawled more frantically than the list on the other side.

    Take care of Bonnie.

Bonnie?

Who, or what, the fuck was Bonnie?

She ripped open the envelope hoping for more clues. Any clue. She stared at the key, mentally swiping through every door she'd ever seen in her life. It wasn't for a lock in their home. If Bonnie were some child from an affair, he couldn't well have hidden her in their house. What had he been hiding from her, and for how long? Would the kids know what he was on about? She was not about to ask them. It wasn't from work. All the doors there were glass, and opened electronically by key card, whooshing past at unnecessary speed. Designed by a man who clearly grew up obsessively watching TV shows set on spaceships. The same architect had designed every separate outbuilding.

    Except one.

xxii.

The heaters roared. Working hard to make it just above cool. January was the harshest month. Where radiators blazed 24 hours a day and ski jackets were worn to the shops. In the dark corridors Thea's footsteps landed like boulders splitting. She looked over her shoulder to make sure she was only being followed by her echoes. She stopped at the door. The metal door so out of place in this world constructed of glass. The design team had talked of air, and light. The Board of Directors spoke of productivity and transparency. Hard to shirk duty if everyone was watching, was the unspoken truth barely kept from their grease-slathered lips. It was an aquarium of people.

For secrets, all you needed was steel.

She fumbled with the key, unmelting ice between her fingers. She tried to keep her breath in as she undid the lock. Flinched as the screech of the hinge filled her ears. And took a step into a room that smelled of brine and something else. Something she thought she knew. An old cologne, rubber, and fish.

In the dimly lit space, she saw Bonnie. She spoke over the loud drum in her chest.

'Hello.'

xxiii.

Thea stepped closer and leaned over the edge. Not too far. The room was as high-tech as any other part of the facility, but something about it seemed old fashioned. Metal and wood, brown tones and no windows shrouded the room in a mystery that tickled the nape of her neck. Most of the room was taken up by water, with only a concrete slab for the desk and computers, and a narrow metal gangway arching around the perimeter. A rusted rainbow. The constant gentle splosh, the heartbeat of the place. The pool was easily twenty metres in diameter. It smelled of salt. This was the part of the complex that jutted out into the mouth of the river. The new mouth, since the piers had been demolished, and the water redirected to suit O.R.C.A.'s needs. Thick metal bars lined the back wall. One was bent and bruised. There must be a cage under the water.

A shadow streaked across her vision. And again. Circling now. Rising up. No longer a shadow.

'You must be Bonnie.'

Thea drank her in. She was beautiful. She'd never seen a thresher up close. The shape of her was something from a child's drawing. So out of proportion yet beautifully crafted for her purpose. Bonnie was magnificent. Sandpaper skin, metallic in its shimmer. Glistening, reflecting any glimmer of light it could catch from the bare lightbulb above her. She had cloudy black eyes, almost mammalian in their coyness. She swam just under the surface of the water, not yet breaking the crust. Six metres long with a small dorsal, almost rounded. Her pectoral fins were gloriously long triangles. Isosceles. Outstretched almost in welcome.

Thea was not a shark expert by any stretch of any imagination, but she had picked up enough from Hector to recognise certain species. Great Hammerheads, naturally, with their unique silhouettes. They swam with them once, stayed low near the seabed and looked up to see sun rays dancing between the school of weaving bodies. Great Whites of course, the epitome of a shark, the first any child would recognise. Whitetips and blacktips had their giveaway colourings – though whitetips could only be found in books nowadays, and she had a soft spot for the peculiarly named porbeagle. Hector had taught her to identify them, catching glimpses of them on the crests of waves, until she could tell one apart from a dolphin with relative ease.

And she knew Bonnie was a thresher because of her tail. A scythe protruding from the back of her long body, another three metres in length. The water frothed as the shark swam in circles, carving the surface into pieces with her reaper's tool. She didn't seem all that happy.

xxiv.

Swinging her legs over the artificial cliff, the one she watched them build as a teenager, she looked down at the people below. The town planners had devised it to a very specific equation. High enough to keep the rising tide back for a few more decades, not so high it would encourage those compelled to jump. Thea had been in so many meetings where the topic of human life was discussed with a cold robotic disconnect. Those bringing up the questions weren't inherently bad. They were just driven by something Thea didn't recognise. Something she hadn't ever taken the wheel of. But there was no avoiding the fact that if they built a suicide hotspot then it would be difficult to market the beaches as a wholesome, family day out with the softest sand in England and the safest water in Europe.

Best to ignore the sand was washed with blood almost daily.

She scoffed lightly. Sure, the water itself was safe. Not too cold, not too hot. Diluted enough that the salt content didn't burn your eyes like parts of the Pacific, which was significantly shallower than it used to be. The freshwater glaciers had finished melting long before they'd reached Southeast Asia. The shape of the Northern English coast meant long open bays, so riptides were rare. You were more likely to hit your head on a surfboard than get pulled out into the deep. For the best, since they'd turned the lifeboat station into a bar café selling inexplicably expensive pastries and 'adult' flavoured ice pops to those who wanted to disguise the fact they needed gin to make them sociable.

It wasn't the beach of her childhood, but she still held affection for the colossal stretch of sand that lined the coastal towns of Newcastle. Dotted with tourists, like ants, 365 days of every year. It had once been three or four separate beaches according to her parents. Bays and harbours split by cliffs and piers thrown out in awkward angular embraces. They shipped in tonnes of fine white sand from overseas, mixed it with the native muddy yellow beach. Made something new and unusual. Devised a USP. Now, you could walk along twenty miles of this unique landscape from the lighthouse ruins that jutted out into the windfarm. Rows and rows of turbines spinning like windmills. All the way down to the fish quay museum, where strings of preserved mackerel shone in air-conditioned glass boxes. Packaged as a beautiful and fascinating display of extinction.

She watched a fin out by the fishing boats. Moving slowly, gracefully, with no resistance at all. A lazy flick of a tail sent ripples to the boats that were anchored a mile out, more for show than for food. Creating that old-world vibe that her team loved so much. People were less likely to complain if they were swaddled in nostalgia. The sea looked ominous, reflecting the gunmetal sky, but it was still. The waves were kitten licks on the sand. A millpond. That's what her father used to say. One of the phrases he continued to use years past the point of understanding, never getting over the fact his grandkids hadn't ever seen a lake.

The fin plunged Thea back to the lab. Back to Bonnie. What an incredible creature she was.

A satchel cut deep into her neck. It was filled with reams of papers swept up from Hector's work desk. Anything that might give her clues as to how the man she had never kept a thing from in nearly two decades had ended up harbouring a secret shark in the River Tyne.

XXV.

'You've cooked?' Mila said, disbelieving.

'Take out.'

'Should've guessed.'

Thea had run out of ways of explaining to Mila that she was trying. That every thought away from how her bruised heart hurt to beat took effort enough to render her unable to get out of bed. To accomplish any task felt Olympian. She hadn't brushed her hair in days but here she was sitting at a table, presenting hot food, with the residue of toothpaste on her gums. She needed someone to recognise the achievement.

'I remembered the naan bread this time.'

She pulled out a chair, encouraging her daughter to join them. Xavier had already torn off a huge chunk of it and was mopping up the spicy soup. He shovelled food into his mouth like he hadn't eaten in days. Had he? If she wasn't cooking, how were the kids eating? She opened her mouth to ask but promptly closed it. Scared of the answers she'd receive. Mila was far more demure in her approach to the meal.

'Is it warm in here?' She shrugged off her coat.

Thea nodded proudly, 'I got us reconnected.'

'Busy day for Mama, hey?' Mila's voice was steady, but the taste of a smile threatened at the corners of her lips.

Thea's hairs stood on end. She hadn't been called Mama in months. She became wrapped in Hector's voice as she ate the last of the steaming rice and watched her children going through the motions of a happy family dinner. Stilted conversations between mouthfuls, arms fighting for space over cooling plates of food.

'Do you two have plans tonight?'

Xavier shook his head. Mila nodded hers.

'I might have to go back to work later. Is that okay Xav?'

Her son looked at her and frowned.

'Fine, yes, it's okay.' She shrugged, feigned nonchalance. She wasn't acting normally; he'd notice if she wasn't careful. Her eyes drifted over to Hector's satchel.

xxvi.

They'd bought that bag on a grey day. The sky so damp and dark it leached colour from everything underneath it. The sea was rippled slate. The white-tipped waves raced each other to crash against the sand. They walked gloved hands entwined, sharing a rare day off together.

    Trying to recall what they'd spoken about was like dredging fossils up from a tar pit. Sticky remnants of words she thought made sense, didn't moments later. She remembered the sky and the sea, the warmth and solidity of his grasp. They'd eaten somewhere, indoors probably given the weather. He'd brushed crumbs from his stubble with a thumb. He'd smelled of sandalwood and coffee. She'd been wearing inappropriate shoes; her toes were prunes when they'd got home.

    She remembered the market but couldn't place where it had been on the map. Didn't know whether they'd driven or caught the train, or whether it was weekend stalls on the beach. A man with a bushy white beard was claiming he sold the best belts in the world. Shark leather belts.

    'Skinned them myself.'

Hector hadn't liked that. Went to examine. The next stall over was selling leather bags. For some reason cow skin didn't bother him so much. Hector had made a show of buying one, a belt too. Thea hadn't seen the bag again, until she noticed it hanging up with his lab coat by the entrance to Bonnie's lair. She'd grabbed it and brought it home.

xxvii.

Papers spilled out across the floor, a tsunami of information. Thea was unsure exactly what she was looking for, there was so much to take in. Hector had documented Bonnie's whole life. What had he missed of her and the kids while his gaze had been shark-shaped?

    She leaned back and rubbed her eye. Stretched out and rolled her shoulders. Bonnie was a research shark but not one bred in captivity. Thea sighed, cast a glance at the spectacular creature and wanted to imagine her patrolling, nothing between her and open ocean except water and light. She'd been an early capture, a few years after Thea had joined the company.

    All that time. Trapped.

    Thea shuddered. Hector had been Bonnie's assigned biologist. What Thea couldn't figure out is when he decided to move her here. Presumably someone higher up had decided she'd had enough, or more likely could be of no more use, and wanted her euthanised. For some reason Hector had decided to spare her.

    Spare.

The official printouts on company headed paper were nowhere to be seen. She'd looked through the satchel twice, rooted in every one of the side pockets, and searched for hidden zips. It wasn't the first time Thea had noticed important documents relating to the exact drugs an animal had been given, lacking or missing completely. Instead, she stared at a piece of paper covered in Hector's hurried scrawl. He'd listed what was presumably everything Bonnie had ever been given. And the effects they were supposed to have. And what those effects had been in actuality.

In the early days, the institute hadn't been so focused on its plan of attack – to make the smell of humans repulsive to sharks. Of course, now they did have that clear goal it was still the sharks that needed to be experimented on. Bred for a life of monitoring and injecting. No humans were ever harmed in the clinical trials. Best to alter the nasal receptors of inferior beasts than the skin cells of the people they were trying to protect. The people who were paying for all this.

The sharks used in the first phase were wild. Plied with drugs to make their teeth brittle so even the new sets that grew to replace them cracked on impact, or their eyesight deadened. Their stomach linings manipulated to vomit if they ate something other than fish. They thrashed in their tanks, bumped into the glass, couldn't eat, their skin flaked off until they bled. On more than one occasion the sharks were found consuming themselves as bloodlust and hunger overcame them.

Bonnie had been through so many trials she was practically blind, and broken teeth clattered in her wide mouth. Each replacement set shattered as they grew. Apparently, she had no sense of smell at all. She wasn't half the creature she could have been. Would have been. Thea sniffed, let the tear roll down her cheek. Two signatures were at the bottom of each new drug development contract. Hector's and someone else's. She couldn't make out the name but whoever it might be was presumably the reason Bonnie hadn't died in Hector's absence.

There was a scrape of metal from the other side of the door. The latch being pulled to one side. Thea turned to marble.

xxviii.

There was nowhere to hide. The door groaned open. Bonnie sensed it too, climbing steadily to the surface, her great tail swishing from side to side. Even though she knew there were no fish, no prey in the tank, something in her coding caused her to switch to hunting mode. She cut through the water as quickly as her small pool allowed. Her dorsal fin rose and dipped in a threatening ballet. Thea started to gather up the papers, moving fast and clumsily, for the first time she wished she wore her prosthetic. Bonnie's thrashing filled her ears, cut the circuits in her brain. Thea knew that Bonnie couldn't harm her on land, but every instinct was tuned in to the 20-foot hunter and was urging her to run.

Something metal hit the floor, chimed. Thea turned and saw the diver from Hector's last boat ride, the one who had come to her house and ruined her life, standing in the doorway. He'd dropped his key at the sight of her, but his own instinct or habit drove him to shut the door immediately, closing them both in. They stared in silence, Thea struggled to remember the last time she had spoken to another adult outside of work or Doctor Reinau's office.

'I see you've met Bonnie,' he broke the silence.

'Hector sent me.' Thea arranged her sweatshirt, not sure of the power dynamic here.

'Wha...'

Thea explained the letter, neglected to say that it was Hector's ritual, his good luck charm. Didn't mention that she kept the pen he'd used on her bedside table.

'What are you going to do?'

'I don't know, Hector was the brains.'

The man didn't look much older than Mila though of course he must be. It was the white coat that aged him, rather than the features on his face.

Bonnie's six-foot sickle of a tail slapped the water, spraying them both.

'Hey Bonbon. It's Lukas.'

Lukas, Thea thought. She stepped out of his way as he started moving quickly, on autopilot. He put his hand in the water, stroked the shark's flank. Speaking calmly the whole time. Asking how her day had been, telling her about his. He walked over to the computer and turned on the screen. The display filled with squares of gloomy underwater

CCTV footage. Each square was a cage. Some empty, others teaming with fish. Lukas tapped furiously on the keyboard.

'The cages are pulled back here, and the fish fill the main tank. That way Bonnie is still able to hunt, and they normally last a day or two if ever we, I, am unable to get back here for a while.'

Hector really had thought of everything hadn't he.

xxix.

'Easy trip in?'

Easier than the morning spent trying to inject a shark with antibiotics and vitamins.

'Sure.'

Dr Reinau frowned; his eyes flicked to the window that was being pelted with hail the size of chickpeas.

'How have you been this week?'

She yawned.

'Busy, or not sleeping?'

Both.

'I sleep fine.'

'Look, Thea. You pay me. If you'd rather be somewhere else, I still get my money.'

She'd never heard him talk like this before. She began to shrug but instead crumpled.

'What do you want to know? That it took me twice as long as it normally does to get here because walking in the snow terrifies me now in case I fall. And I only have myself to blame for that. And I know I could wear the arm, but I don't want to. I don't want to learn how to use something new. Of course I'm going to wear it at some point, but that is the next part of my life and I'm not ready for the next part of my life because I never wanted to say goodbye to the old part of my life. I never got to say goodbye to the old part. I miss my old life. I miss him. I miss him so much that I still wear his clothes. I still talk to him. I miss him so much I can't breathe. I still haven't changed our sheets. Isn't that disgusting? I haven't moved on even an inch.'

Thea took a deep breath.

'I feel like I'm drowning. Except it's worse because at least if you drown, it ends.'

Doctor Reinau sighed, tilted his head. 'Yes. I want to know all that.'

XXX.

For the sixteenth or seventeenth time that week Thea was in Hector's lab. She was attempting Dr Reinau's homework. He wanted her to write a letter to Hector. She thought sitting in his chair with his white coat draped across the back would help. She held the cuff between her thumb and forefinger. The pristine sheet of paper still on his desk. Bonnie swam up and down, round and round. Completely institutionalised. For the sixteenth or seventeenth time that week Thea played out various possible scenarios for Bonnie's escape. Would she survive? Would a few weeks as a free animal be better than years in a cage? What happened if she or Lukas grew bored, needed to move away? Would Bonnie even want to leave? Could she tell Hector was gone? Why did she care?

Her phone buzzed in her pocket. Xav.

'Mila made me ring because you'd be more likely to answer.'

Thea opened her mouth to protest but they were probably right. For Xav to pick up the phone there was usually a genuine problem. If Mila was dialling it could be anything from lost keys, only one slice of bread left, or the more probable empty purse syndrome.

'Mam, are you coming home this evening?'

'Of course.'

'You sure? You've barely been home all week.'

'What are you talking about?'

Mila whittered about not coming in until the early hours, leaving the door open, no food in the fridge.

'Aren't you an adult too?' Thea snapped, instantly regretting it.

Mila hung up. The silence rang like a bell.

When was the last time she'd seen the kids' faces? Asked how they were doing? When was the last time she'd seen daylight? She picked up the pen and put it straight back down again.

xxxi.

'What's wrong?' Lukas asked, not looking up. His dark hair was damp, the team had been on a dive that morning. Releasing treated shark pups back into the wild. The team would return in a week to see if any had survived, how they'd integrated.

Thea was pacing, rubbing her arm. She'd forgotten a meeting. A big meeting. A big meeting with a new investor. And now she had a new meeting. To explain why she had left their most important client hanging around the foyer for an hour without an explanation. She didn't think that the true explanation would be good enough. That she had replaced the man she loved with a shark. And that watching that shark swim around in circles was as close to spending time with him as she was ever going to get again. That she read years-old research each night instead of sleeping, hoping to find a way to reverse everything that had been done to the wretched creature so she could be set free.

Which she?

'Nothing. I'll sort it.'

'Want to see something cool?' Lukas was trying to distract her, like she used to with the kids when they were little.

She forced her tongue down from the roof of her mouth.

'Cooler than the pet thresher I seem to have inherited?'

Lukas shrugged. 'We can find someone else.'

'No,' she shouted, an octave too loud.

She walked over to him, 'what do you want to show me?'

She placed her hand between his shoulder blades. Felt warm. Solid. Lukas tensed. She moved it, felt hot.

Idiot.

xxxii.

Thea was underwater. She often dreamt that she was underwater, waking in a tangle of damp sheets gasping for breath. But here she was calm. She could breathe. A mermaid of sorts. Her hair floated around her, cast jellyfish shadows in the crystal flecked shallows. She kicked her legs, moved easily. Let the coolness wash over her, seep into the fire that blazed in her chest. Music was playing, an old clockwork toy. Mechanic, echoing.

Lies over the ocean

Lies over the sea

Bring back, bring back

Everything was bathed in sunlight, pale blue glitter cutting through her saltwater womb. She looked around, she seemed alone in this tranquil pool. Then a shadow. Her heart quickened, just a little. She laid back, floated. Her stomach was melted chocolate. The sun burned violet, turned grey. A full moon.

Below her, Bonnie appeared. Her giant tail cocooning Thea's head.

Swept away to the left.

Swept up from the right.

Allegro downwards, a spiral.

Thrown upwards with fierce speed.

Caught without a ripple.

Plié.

Embrace.

Arabesque, mirror Bonnie.

Stretch taut.

Pain easily pinpointed.

Pain to fight through.

Sissonne slices the water.

In pieces.

Thea was lost. But not alone.

The moon was a dot and light couldn't penetrate, but even in the deepest ocean Thea could still see Bonnie. Only Bonnie.

xxxiii.

Dear Hector,

~~Why did you choose her?~~

~~I've been told to write this letter~~

~~I want to write this letter~~

You used to write letters. I don't know how you ever found the words. Where have they gone? I remember I used to be smart. But you aren't the only thing that left me. I'm not who I used to be. You did that to me. I sound so angry I know, I should apologise. ~~I will when you do.~~

~~We always taught the kids not to keep secrets.~~

~~The kids want to speak about you.~~ We miss you. The house is quieter now. Mila got into university. Xav got a job. ~~I've forgotten what it is.~~ He's busy at least.

Remember the time we went out on the boat and he got seasick? I was preoccupied looking for a dolphin or a seal. In that moment I wished that we were on that boat alone, snuggled under a blanket watching the shimmer of the waves and the sinking sun and enjoying animals ~~that didn't want to eat us~~ for them, not for work. I threw a tantrum while you mopped him up. I would have stormed off that boat if I could. A grown woman. Pathetic. You made him feel safe. Mila was clinging to your arm too, wasn't she? You looked after both of them so effortlessly. It came so easily to you. I'm not so sure they feel safe right now, I'm too busy watching the water and no one's steering the boat, Hector. We're rudderless. Hurled across a seething ocean and I don't know where the life jackets are. ~~You stole the lifejackets.~~

~~Did we ever have any?~~

When you left, the ground turned to water. It feels dangerous to tread.

I don't know how to be.

I still love you. ~~But I hate you.~~

xxxiv.

'I think Bonnie likes you,' Lukas was looking at charts that made no sense to Thea.

'Don't be absurd. How can you tell?'

'She just seems happier, healthier.'

'Coincidence.'

Thea looked over at the pool. The water was agitated, disturbed by ripples from the wild storm that raged.

'How does she cope with the thunder and lightening?'

'Spends more time deeper down, bangs against the cage a bit.'

How can that be right?

'Do you ever think about just letting her go?'

Lukas didn't turn round but stopped clicking the mouse.

'All the time.'

'Then why don't we?'

The taste of freedom was caramel on her tongue. To return to a normal life, to forget this room existed.

And lose the last piece of Hector?

Lukas turned to look at her. Dark circles under his eyes, hair not been cut for months. His freckles receding. He sighed a sigh of a much older man. When had Hector brought the young technician in to help care for Bonnie? Thea knew his responsibility had doubled now he was the only biologist. She did what she could, had learnt how to operate the feeds and helped with medication when she could, but they both knew she was observing more than contributing.

'How often do O.R.C.A. send out boats to monitor the population? Even if she survived in open waters, she'd be discovered so soon and brought back in for testing. No way they'd see a shark in that state and not want to dig around. We'd be caught almost as quickly as her.'

'You said she'd been getting healthier.'

'She still looks like a test shark though, Thee.'

The wind was knocked from her. The word a mallet.

Thee.

She imagined Hector casually talking about her and the kids, their pet names soaking into these dank walls.

Lukas hadn't noticed, 'she might as well be branded with Hector's name.'

Thea looked around the room. 'This is our lot then?'

'She's getting on. She won't last forever.' He sounded more hopeful that certain.

'How long do they live?'

'There's never been one in captivity before.'

'How old is she now?'

'Late teens.'

'Great, three teenagers to look after.'

Lukas offered a weak smile.

'I am trying.'

'Oh, I know.' A proper smile. 'I'm glad I'm not doing this alone, even if you do have to bring your bad jokes.'

XXXV.

'You seem,' the doctor paused, his mouth puckering as it searched for the right word, 'well.'

A lie, she'd caught sight of herself in the mirror that hung in the reception. She nodded, attempted a smile. She checked her watch. Her eyes stung from lack of sleep.

'Somewhere to be?' His eyes were scanning, trying to read her. He'd long since put down his notebook. Thea hadn't spoken much today. She couldn't concentrate. Couldn't stop thinking about Bonnie. What was she going to do with her? She couldn't carry on like this. Dr Reinau was sitting with his hands resting in his lap. He wore the same beige trousers he always did. He leaned forward. Opened his palms out toward her. Some dumb psychologist trick, he's open, inviting. Encouraging her to talk.

'No. Course not.'

'I think it's fair to say you have something on your mind.'

She scoffed. Jiggled her foot. Her stomach bubbled; blood simmered. She itched to scream at Hector. To tell him how hard all this had been. To ask how he'd managed, how he'd even considered, keeping this secret from her that whole time. Why he'd thought she'd be up to this task? But most of all she wanted to talk to someone. She was exhausted of being mute.

'I'm just so tired, the kids seem to need me as much as they did when they were toddlers and then there's Bon...'

Dr Reinau sat back, reached for his notebook. Tried not to look too eager.

'Who?'

Shit.

Her palms became marshes.

'No one.'

'You were talking about people who take up so much of your time. But it's no one?'

Thea wilted, her mind racing.

Dr Reinau frowned. 'Have you met someone?'

Thea scrunched her face up, the thought of being with someone new repulsive. Quickly dissolved the scorn into a grimace. Hoped it looked enough like a smile.

'Yes. Yes, I've met someone.'

'I see.'

'You sound surprised.'

You aren't the only one.

'I'm not surprised,' he swirled the word around his mouth like a piece of chocolate he'd challenged himself not to chew, 'it's just very soon. You haven't given any indication in our sessions that you were ready for that. You haven't even given much indication that you fully accept that Hector's gone,' he arched an eyebrow.

'Just sort of happened.' She raised her hand up, tried to appear natural and at ease rather than entangled in a lie. About to be swept into wide open jaws.

'Does he know about Hector?'

'Hector introduced us.'

Her shoulders unclenched and no longer lingered by her ears. She took a deep breath. Smelled lavender. Synthetic oil, but a good replica. Spritzed in doctor's offices around the country. Still had the calming effect the plant used to. Dr Reinau didn't need to know her new partner was a thresher shark. He wasn't going to ask that; she wasn't going to get found out here.

'Excuse me? Are you still talking to Hector?' His pencil twitched on the paper.

'Every day,' she brushed off his look of concern, 'but that's not what I mean.'

He shuffled in his chair. Losing patience with her. Brushed imaginary crumbs off his knee.

'They were a friend of Hector's.'

'I see.'

'We sort of got thrown together by losing him. I think she understands.'

'You speak like she was in love with Hector.'

'She might have been, in her own way.' Thea was losing him, she laughed lightly, shook her head. 'Everyone loved Hector.'

'Are you ready to tell me about him?'

Thea's tongue turned to lead. Teeth clenched.

'Maybe next time.'

xxxvi.

Condensation rolled down the glass. The ice cubes, slowly melting, clinked against each other. She hadn't realised the music had been switched off until she heard the gentle clatter of the ice. She looked up; they were the only two people in the pub. The barman was reading on a stool. She couldn't remember the last time one of them had got up to order a drink. She smiled across the table.

Hector spoke animatedly. Their conversation had long departed from work. He was describing a sandwich he'd once eaten, with the passion of a Shakespearian actor. He even closed his eyes when he described the salad. Thea couldn't help but notice the thickness of his eyelashes. She couldn't think of a meal that had ever stirred such strong feelings in her, let alone cold meats shoved between two slices of bread.

The team meeting had run on way past the regular end of day. There had been a communications catastrophe over the weekend as the social channels were unattended and only scheduled posts had appeared. The facility was boasting a breakthrough, headed up by bright young thing – Hector no less – allowing for the safest summer yet. Minutes after they shared their news, a family's rubber dinghy had been attacked by a tiger shark. Mum, Dad and three kids. Thea shuddered. She watched the man in front of her, he cared so strongly about the creatures back in the facility's tanks, but his eyes welled when he spoke of the family who'd just lost their lives. There was so much emotion in him. Thea felt glacial in his presence.

    The team had spent all afternoon revising then releasing a statement. One that was apologetic but hopeful. Mournful but avoided hyperbole. Tone was everything. They'd eaten their evening meals in the office, rescheduled date nights, arranged babysitters, cancelled plans. Their boss never asked much of her staff beyond regular work hours but expected no complaints on the occasions it did happen. One by one the rest had dropped away, leaving Thea with Hector. The fast-rising junior lab technician and the lowliest comms executive. She'd never paid him much attention before now. She had no idea why.

    He squeezed her arm as he stepped by her, his hand was warm. Without thinking she lifted her own hand to touch where his had just been. She checked over her shoulder to watch him walk to the toilets. Funny how much you could see when someone wasn't wearing a knee-length coat.

She ordered two drinks from the barman, who placed his book face down by a pile of beermats advertising boat trips out to the Grotto. Guaranteed sharks.

Hector came up behind her and placed his hands on her hips, whispered in her ear.

'Is this okay?'

'Very.'

They shared the air all night.

xxxvii.

'Did Bonnie know Hector well?'

    'You could say that.'

    'Were they romantically involved?'

    'No, I shouldn't have thought so.'

    'Were you aware of their friendship?'

    No.

    'Do you want to talk about the fact Bonnie is a woman?'

    'Does that matter?'

    'Only if it does to you.'

    'That's got nothing to do with anything.'

    Her sessions had become repetitive. Dr Reinau asked her about coping with her day-to-day life – had the kids had a nutritious meal in the last week? Had she? Was she sleeping, washing, laughing, crying? Had she had another episode of forgetting the way to work? Did she still dream that the children would drown too? How was her physical health? Had she managed to see friends that week? She threw him a bone, mentioned Lukas. Then he asked about Bonnie. She was quite enjoying making up, *lying*, little stories about her new – not at all unhealthy or unnatural – relationship. It was easier than telling the truth, which she hadn't really figured out how to articulate yet.

She didn't know whether she would ever want to, or feel ready to, be with another person ever again. Caring for an elderly fish and pretending to be in love with her was much easier.

xxxviii.

The team had suggested she take a day off. She didn't believe it was entirely altruistic. She was fully aware that she hadn't been pulling her weight in the office. Staring blankly at a computer screen no longer constituted as work. Flashes of fevered productivity every week or so were the only thing keeping her out of the Boardroom. People's patience with the grieving widow was wearing thin.

A year should be enough for anyone.

What did they know? Obviously, none of them had ever had the carpet pulled from underneath them. Sending them rolling backwards down a hill that never flattens out. Breaking every bone on the way down, never finding the time to rest and heal. Too busy gathering speed. So what if they had to pick up a little debris?

She had spent the morning moving things around her house. Not tidying, just busying her hands. After attempting to rearrange the room by moving the armchair, stubbornly refusing to slide the prosthetic over her elbow, she admitted defeat. Left the chair where it was, now on its side. Sweating, she left the house and walked towards the sea, but she grew heavier, slowed with every step. She didn't want to look at water. Didn't want to smell salt or sun cream. Didn't need to hear any screams.

xxxix.

'Help!' Lukas cried out, the roar erupting from him, his eyes lost in panic. Impossible to tell what colour they were as the pupils had eclipsed them. He was in the water, caught by Bonnie's tail, a whip, as he'd peered in, checking whether she could still cope with hunting. The shoal of fish darted through the water, desperate to avoid the two killers thrashing amongst them. Bonnie's dorsal fin dipped below the water. Thea's legs went numb, unable to get up from where she'd landed. She dragged herself forward, felt like she was moving through mud. Lukas's arms were crashing against the water as he grabbed for the side of the tank, just out of his reach. His hand slapped against the smooth metal surface. It didn't matter whether he splashed or not now, Bonnie was in a lather. She plucked off a fish or two. Guts gleamed in the murky water. Lukas screamed as she brushed by him, ducking below him.

Thea hurled herself forward, had to grab onto a rail to stop herself going in right after him.

'Grab my arm.'

She cursed every decision she'd made in the last 13 months, stretched herself as far as her bones could to reach him. He scrabbled, scratching, at her tender silver scars, turning them scarlet. She winced, fought every instinct to flinch. To flee.

Bonnie launched herself at Lukas, pushed him up through the water, his white coat now the colour of a sunset. Deep burning red. His face was ash, his eyes rolled back into his head. He howled.

'Lukas.' Thea shrieked, piercing his shock.

He lunged forward, grabbed her arm, her shoulder, her hair. Had fistfuls of her. She pulled back as sharply as she could. Every muscle shouting at her. Screaming. Lukas deafening her. She didn't know if it was his tears or hers that she could taste.

The two of them huddled together on the stone floor while Bonnie returned to hunting fish, her flanks raising and falling with exertion. Lukas's blood swirled downwards towards the riverbed, a ruby fog. Thea didn't need to look at it, she was already sinking.

xl.

'What are you doing?'

'Do you want me to stop?'

'No,' Lukas's voice was small, crumbled stone. Thea stroked the smooth skin between his eyebrows with her thumb. She hummed an old lullaby.

'You're in the hospital.'

Lukas nodded, barely moving his head. 'What did you tell them?' His lips cracked as he spoke.

'That we were swimming and you got bitten.' She didn't mention that she'd dragged him through the building to the riverside. Terrified that he would fall to pieces before she got him out. Or that she was due in an emergency meeting to discuss how best to warn the public about sharks that now seemingly patrolled the river at night.

xli.

'What are you doing?'

'Do you want me to stop?'

'No,' Hector's voice dripped with honey. On his back, dark hair splayed out over the pillow.

'What shall we do today?'

'Stay here,' his eyes closed again. She lay her head against his chest, felt his heartbeat inside her. Felt hot gentle breath parting her hair.

She placed a hand on her stomach, couldn't tell yet but there was something growing. Someone. She wanted to tell him, but she wanted to let him sleep more.

'You're going to be a dad,' she whispered.

He sighed in his sleep, pulled her closer.

She sighed wide awake, pulled his arm around her tighter.

xlii.

She ducked under the police tape flapping in the breeze. Bleached bone white by years in the sun, it cordoned off the old nature reserve. Once a quarry, then a sanctuary, now a memorial. The trees and plants had dried so fast they didn't have time to rot. Everything preserved, overground fossils. Gulls circled above but never landed. Thea walked, enjoying the heavy quiet. Couldn't remember when she'd last breathed this deeply.

She followed the path up the gentle slope. Every patch of earth, every crisp blackberry bush threw memories at her. Feeding the ducks, picnics hours before lunchtime, wellies in muddy puddles, climbing trees.

She looked at the gnarled branches of the sycamore leaning out over the parched quarry pit. Once framing a reservoir below, now only cracked mud could be seen between its outstretched limbs. She reached out, felt the rough bark beneath her fingers. She pushed harder, still felt solid enough. She kicked the roots. Placed her feet in the same knots the kids had used when they were small. She pushed up, grabbed the only thing she could reach, a palmful of dusty leaves. They disintegrated and snowed down on her as she fell backwards and hit the ground.

    Glad no one was around, she brushed herself off. Tried again. She tried until she was exhausted. Panting and sweating, she blamed the tree, the shoes, the heat. Wouldn't admit the real reason she couldn't get up a trunk she'd climbed thousands of times before.

xliii.

The day had been hot. So hot the sun had stripped the top layer of the ocean, a scab peeled off a tender wound, caused a mist that hid the horizon. So hot, even once the sun had set the air was still stew. Thea tugged the padded duvet out from between the cover. She still hadn't changed the bedding. The idea of washing him away made her feel like stale bread. Hard, and only good for crumbs. She dumped the padding on the floor. A thin film of moisture beaded her forehead. The exertion of this small movement enough to melt her.

She drew Hector's pillow into her. Yellowed, flattened, frayed. She gulped him in. Felt the sting behind her eyes, allowed herself one memory. Walking through a garden, close but not holding hands. Hector stooping to smell the flowers. She drifted to sleep, snared in a net of sheets.

She dreamt of Bonnie. Muscles flexing as she circled, blue grey flanks flashing. Her tail swayed and thrashed more violently with every flick. Grew bigger, sharper. Her skin melted into chiffon. A gown. Bonnie was a woman. A grey leather jacket that was rough to the touch. She had dark eyes and a kind smile. Silver hair, long down to the floor and trailing behind her like a wedding train, curved and ending in a point. She kissed Thea's forehead then her neck. Traced her spine with gentle tapping fingers. She held her hips and circled her thumbs over the bones. She leant in and licked the scars on her arm. Bared her teeth and

xliv.

Thea heard crying from the kitchen. Mila had her head buried in her arms, her back danced with grief. Thea rushed towards her, a breaker wave.

'What is it?'

Mila shook her off, wiped her eyes.

'Didn't know you were in.'

'Love, please.'

Mila sniffed; her hair matted to her face. Thea reached out, untangled the mess with her fingers.

'I know anniversaries are tough.'

'It's not that.'

'What then?' Thea still had ink on her fingers. She'd written him a birthday card, slipped it inside an envelope and sealed it shut. Slid it into his desk.

'You'll think it's silly.'

'I don't think anything that makes you this upset could be silly.'

Xav appeared in the doorway, Thea waved him away. He stayed, pulled up a chair.

'Is it Noah?'

'Who's Noah?'

Mila nodded.

How much had she missed?

'He's seeing someone else.'

Thea watched her daughter's face fold in on itself and wanted more than anything to take that pain away. To hurl it across the ocean, too far out to return on the tide. Let the salt eat it. She squeezed her girl's hand. Mila let her, her frost dissolving like seafoam.

'That's not silly at all. Someone you trusted hurt you. I'm not sure there's a worse feeling. To believe one thing and for something else entirely to be true is enough to rip your heart out.'

Xav frowned. Mila blinked, thick eyelashes studded with dew.

'To think about that one person, who you trusted more than anyone else, putting something else before you. Choosing to spend short precious time with someone else when you'd never even considered taking your eyes off them.' Her voice rose as she fought to stay calm. 'To never understand what was going through their head, or to hear an explanation. To never hear an apology.'

She stopped, reached out to cup her daughter's face in her hand, whispered, 'well that must be torture.'

Four chairs housed three silent bodies. Thea stared into the space at the table, wondered what she might say if it was occupied.

xlv.

Wincing, Thea dug her nails into the bark. The bruises still throbbed from the last time she'd tried. She sneered at herself and the notion that she could do this.

Drizzle hung like fish scales dispersed in a feeding frenzy or cast into the air by a monger's knife. The damp made her heavier. The tangled branches swayed, taunting her.

'It would be much easier if you had this.'

Thea gasped, just managed to stop herself grabbing at her chest like a Hollywood starlet. Her cry, an echo in the deserted quarry. She slid down the rough wood, grazing her palm. Xav stood gawkishly, holding out her arm.

Had he followed her? How many times?

'I don't need it.'

He sighed, fed up. 'You do if you want to sit in that tree.'

'You could be helpful and give me a leg up.'

He pondered the arm, the exact colour of his mother's skin but as detached from her as the moon.

'Fine.' He placed the limb down carefully.

With a boost, Thea felt briefly like she was flying. A grunt from her young son and she was seated, legs swaying like they were laughing. She inhaled deeply through her nose, smelled decay.

'Thank you.'

Xav spoke to the floor, to his awkwardly large feet, to the dust. 'You don't have to make everything harder for yourself.'

'I don't.'

He looked at her, not that dissimilarly to Dr Reinau. 'Dad's gone now, and you might have to start doing some stuff by yourself. I can't always follow you round cleaning up.'

Cleaning up?

'Xav, I…'

'It's fine, you've been,' he paused, 'preoccupied.'

He hoisted the prosthetic into a jumble of branches.

'What are you doing?' Thea called. But he didn't turn back as he left her in the tree. There was only one way she could get herself down safely.

xlvi.

'Who is this guy again?' Mila asked, her hair now shoulder length, dank and needing a cut. Thea had thought about suggesting she go to a salon, offer to pay for it. A treat, something restorative for her girl. She held back though, knew very well how that conversation would go. Her own hair was shorn. Preferable to dealing with stilted conversation in a sticky leather chair, with a woman she didn't want to make eye contact with. Xav had cut it over the bath a few weeks ago, humouring his mother's breakdown but not enough to hand over the razor. No one spoke to her about it. Dr Reinau cast a glance and wrote something down, nothing more. She liked it, liked the feel of it, smooth like silk in one direction, bristly like stubble in the other. Liked that when she brushed her hair now, she wasn't reminded of Lukas screaming every time the comb got caught in a lug.

    They were setting the table for four. Lukas was coming round for some food, a small celebration before his imminent return to work. Thea had attempted to bake a cake. Mila was standing, looking down into the bin where said cake now resided, trying to figure out who this man was that her mother felt compelled to cook for.

'A friend from work,' Thea placed emergency shop-bought biscuits on a plate, sliced fresh bread from the bakery and checked the soup – the one thing she did know how to cook – bubbling on the hob.

'Why all the effort?' Xav stared at the table, laid with matching plates and clean cutlery.

'He's been through a lot.'

'Oh yeah,' Mila said as she left the room, 'where was our cake?'

xlvii.

'Are you sure?'

Lukas had come into the room, announced by the squeal of the door. Thea really had not expected to see him back there. He limped in on a crutch, looked stiff. She forced down the memory of the last time she'd seen him on that gangway.

He eyed the water, didn't sit down.

'Had to at some point, didn't I?'

'Not if you didn't want to.'

'But who would...'

She didn't let him finish, 'I think it's time we let her go. Lukas, it's got to be time.'

He wrenched his eyes away from the pool to look at Thea. His head was shaking.

'We can't.'

'Imagine your life without her.'

Thea imagined her own. So much time, so much freedom.

So much loneliness.

'I'm not sure I can.'

'We need to try.'

He hung his head, 'it feels like letting Hector down.'

'I know,' Thea took his hand, 'but do you ever stop to think about how Hector let you down? Let me down?'

'He was doing what he felt was right.'

'For who?'

'Bonnie.'

'Well, I think it's maybe our turn.'

xlviii.

The date on the paper burned. 15 July. Dive cancelled. Thea kept reading, expecting the number to change. It couldn't be. If the dive was cancelled, then why was Hector in the water?

She'd only nipped in to tidy up, so Lukas didn't come in on Monday to her mess. Quick scoop up of all her clutter, chuck it in the satchel and try and forget about it over the weekend. Mila had planned a day out for them. Thea had been too shocked by this to argue and say no. Xav had tried it, but his sister had worn him down.

Shoving the metal door closed, she marched to find Lukas. Her clenched fist swinging, propelling her. She spotted him through a window. Looking down a microscope, concentrating. She slammed her hand against the glass, a short fizz of power tickled her spine as she watched him jump and flush red. Her face warned him she was not going to wait long.

'We need to talk,' she said as soon as the sliding door swooshed closed. Every other person in the lab was craning their necks, looking curiously at each other. Unable to figure out what someone from the senior team would want with a lab rat. She gave them a cool little wave, reminded them that it was a window, and she could see them. They scurried, cartoonish, back to work.

His face had drained. His eyes wouldn't settle, wouldn't look directly at Thea.

'You know what this is about don't you?'

'I've been waiting.'

'Coward. Why didn't you just tell me?'

'How could I tell you, Thee? You've spent so much time helping me, you obviously care for her. How am I supposed to casually drop into conversation that Bonnie killed Hector?'

Lukas was still talking, Thea could see his mouth moving, but his words were drowned out by a rumble, tanks advancing, grenades in the distance. Like she was standing under a waterfall, water hitting her, bruising her, crushing her. She blinked, tried to bring the room back into focus. She licked her lips with a tongue rough as sharkskin. Bonnie had killed Hector? The same Bonnie she had spent months protecting, figuring out a way to save. The Bonnie who had glided into her dreams.

Lukas wringed his hands, placing them in and out of his pockets, rubbing his forearm. Thea felt dizzy watching him. She grabbed him, tried to steady herself.

'That isn't what you wanted to talk about was it?' His voice less than a whisper.

'I knew the dive had been cancelled.' Her own voice seemed loud, bouncing around the white corridor. Smashing itself into her ears.

'I'm so sorry.' He wobbled.

'You don't get to faint.' She offered no hint of kindness.

'Can we get a drink?'

xlix.

Lukas hadn't touched his tea. It had stopped steaming. Thea's own cup was empty, and the sugary liquid stagnated in her stomach. She knew it wasn't going to last long inside her. She shook as beads of sweat ran down her back and temples. She felt like she had the flu. But she knew this wasn't the flu. Shock had rewired her.

Hector had cancelled the dive last minute. It had always been the plan, apparently. Bonnie's cage needed attention and he needed to create time to fix it. She'd bent one of the girders. Testament that even in her fragile state she was a beast who could weaken metal as easily as fire.

'Why didn't he just let her escape?'

'Hector knew she wouldn't survive.'

'So what? He chose her life over his?'

Lukas fidgeted in his seat. At least now he had a cup to hold, his hands had stopped flailing around. Thea had thought she was going to get motion sickness as they'd walked to the café.

'He obviously didn't think she...' He trailed off, almost in disbelief.

'I need you to tell me exactly what happened.'

Lukas shook his head, opened his mouth in protest.

'Look at me, Lukas. Look at me.' She held her arm out, noted that he didn't react to her scars anymore. Instead, he looked at them like they were giving him permission. 'I'm already broken. You can't hurt me more than I already am.'

Sure about that?

Hector had decided to fix the cage, it wasn't the first time he'd swum with Bonnie, so he was confident. Complacent. He still suited up with the chainmail over his wetsuit, but he was jovial in a way he never was before a regular dive out in open water. He slid into the pool slowly, carefully. Bonnie didn't seem bothered by him. He sank down, started work. Lukas had stayed on dry land, working the machinery, and keeping an eye on Hector's oxygen levels.

Before Lukas had registered what was happening, Bonnie rushed at Hector. Her half toothless jaws open, her nearly-blind eyes focused. She used her tail to stun him.

Like he was a fucking herring.

And then she bit down. Hector's breath was stolen from him as she clamped her teeth, sharp as blades, around his equipment, puncturing the oxygen tube. Snapped off in the rubber. Shattered teeth adding to the carnage.

Not to worry, your missing pieces grow back.

Lukas said he still sees the stream of bubbles dwindling in the water before he falls asleep at night. Thea said she would now.

'How did you get him back?'

Lukas explained how he had lured Bonnie away with chum, a rain of blood and guts no shark could ignore. Bonnie's dead food came with an electronic pulse she could sense. Used at times when shoals wouldn't be found in Northern waters. She had dropped Hector like a dog bored of a toy.

'Had she been fed before he went in?'

'Of course.' Lukas looked offended.

'Then why would she attack?'

His chin still bore the mottled scars of teenage acne beneath black stubble. She sighed. Lukas had a whole life ahead of him, a life in which he would fall in love. Would feel that electric spark at a first touch. Would share secrets across a dark bed. Would watch that person change and age, thicken their bark like an oak.

It's not fair.

'I'm sorry, I just don't know.'

1.

The silence had been going on too long, Thea knew that. Dr Reinau blinked slowly, was giving her room to speak. She'd just admitted Bonnie was dangerous. He'd asked how. Predatory, she'd said. Possessive. When she gets something between her teeth she doesn't let go.

'Sounds like it's stopped being fun.'

That was the last thing he'd said. Thea rested in the quiet, a marshmallow wrapped around her. She wondered if it ever had been fun.

Half her session ticked by without another word.

'I think,' Dr Reinau's expression didn't change as she finally spoke, 'the only reason I liked her was because she was a link to Hector.'

The doctor nodded slowly, 'yes.'

'Was that obvious to you?'

'That's not for me to say.'

'I still miss him.'

'Of course you do.'

'Every time I hear a door or floorboard creak, I think it's him. I forget it can't be.'

'Because you haven't allowed yourself to properly process his death. You immediately distracted yourself with work, with Bonnie. You had other things to concentrate on.' He gestured to her arm.

'You can say the words.'

'Your way of coping has been distraction, and I am not sure that has worked.'

'Would you like to know about him?'

li.

'You weren't going to tell me?' Thea scoffed. She knew she should be pleased for him. Lukas leant on his crutch.

'Didn't know how.'

'But a note?' She thrust the scrap of paper under his nose, remembered the last note she'd been left.

'I wasn't thinking.' He twisted. Ran a hand through his hair.

'That would be more convincing if you weren't smiling.'

'I'm just excited.'

Thea paced in the small space. She should hug him, congratulate him. A new job. A new home, inland. A fresh start.

'I never thought I'd want to move away from the sea.'

'What am I going to do?'

'What you've said you're going to the whole time.'

'Let her go?'

'Let her go.'

Serve her right

Bonnie slapped the water, as if she sensed Thea's turn in mood. Lukas jumped. Clutched the crutch with two hands. He seemed to shrink. Thea still hadn't brought herself to look at the shark. Dragged herself in to release a shoal so it didn't starve. But maybe the wretched thing deserved to die.

'You need to go.' Thea said softly, recognising the rise of tears creeping. She reached out to give his arm a squeeze. Remind him he was on solid ground. 'We'll be fine.'

lii.

The waves spat red onto the sand. The surf's bubbles were thick with blood. A soup. No one could see the source. Where was it coming from? How was it still coming? It was impossible to tell. Water and seaweed churned and dispersed the gore until it was no more. In less than a minute the tide had swallowed the scene. Onlookers gathered in the shallows, checked around their ankles for clues. Desperate not to find anything. A few shouted they could taste pennies.

Thea noticed the crowd as her bare feet sunk into the wet sand. The clump of people stood out on the slowly darkening bay. The beach tried to swallow her every step, dragging at her heels. She licked her lips, tasted the iron-rich mist. She considered a jog, a run, a retreat. She didn't want to confirm what she already knew. What made the faded scar tissue at her elbow tingle and itch. What was going to cause her team endless hours of overtime tomorrow. She started a second lap of the bay with a heavy pant, walking was difficult in this heat. Sweat nipped at her eyes, the air was thick enough to spread, hard to breathe.

A scream curdled the clouds.

A stampede from the water, people flung down in their rush to escape the shallows.

Thea sat in the sand, watched the scene unfold. There was nothing she could do. The emergency services would already be on their way. The horizon whipped around her, shimmered and blinded. She closed her eyes, lay back in the sand. Had she always been this exhausted?

liii.

Weight shifted on the bed, caused Thea to wake with a start. Heart bruising, she didn't express her disappointment at seeing the children perched by her feet.

'Happy birthday.'

Is it?

'You had no idea, did you?'

She picked crust from the corner of her eye, smiled without teeth. 'I'm sure if I'd checked a calendar, I would've figured it out.'

She looked at them both, hurtling towards adulthood. Couldn't remember the last time she'd wrapped them a present. Hector was always in charge of that. She supplied the means; he served the sentiment in ladles. Always got it right.

'I missed yours.'

Shrugs and the awkward push of a neatly wrapped gift towards her.

liv.

'I'm sorry,' she whispered. Again, louder. Again, until she was shouting. She exhaled, tasted salt on her lips. 'I don't want to say goodbye.'

The walls closed in, squeezed the air out of her. Thea collapsed onto the floor. Bonnie's fin rose to the surface, slit the water like a scalpel. Silent. Deadly. Tired.

So tired.

Thea closed her eyes, saw Hector. Watched him button a shirt, wash a glass, comb Mila's hair, kiss Xav's grazed knee. She saw him lean close, brush her cheek. She saw him swim with Bonnie.

Bonnie.

Thea watched the huge body writhe. Thea knew how she felt, too big for her space. Put there by a man's terrible decision. By Hector's good intentions.

Good for who exactly?

Finally, she felt clear about what she had to do. She heaved herself up and made her way to the computer.

She watched the screen flicker, the temperature, tide times, feeding schedule. Everything was there. Everything Hector had worked so hard for. Everything, he'd kept secret from her. Chosen over her.

Then there was the cage release. Thea's finger hovered over the command. She knew Bonnie might not survive long out there.

She might though.

But she knew they couldn't both survive if Bonnie stayed in this cage, and she stayed in hers.

It wasn't really Bonnie she needed to say goodbye to.

The clock ticked.

The water lapped.

Bonnie thrashed.

Thea decided.

And undecided.

All it would take is the click of a mouse.

When she was ready.

When I'm ready.

Her finger hovered.

Martha Lane is a writer by the sea. She writes extensively about love, loss and all things unrequited, many of her stories can be found online at marthalane.co.uk.

Printed in Great Britain
by Amazon

21491722R00078